First American Edition 2015
Kane Miller, A Division of EDC Publishing

Text copyright © 2014 Sally Rippin
Illustrations copyright © 2014 Aki Fukuoka

First published in Australia by Hardie Grant Egmont 2014

All rights reserved, including the rights of reproduction
in whole or in part in any form.

For information contact:
Kane Miller, A Division of EDC Publishing
P.O. Box 470663
Tulsa, OK 74147-0663
www.kanemiller.com
www.edcpub.com
www.usbornebooksandmore.com

Library of Congress Control Number: 2014945690

Printed and bound in the United States of America
2 3 4 5 6 7 8 9 10
ISBN: 978-1-61067-364-8

A Billie B. MYSTERY

Strawberry Thief

By Sally Rippin

Illustrated by Aki Fukuoka

Kane Miller

A DIVISION OF EDC PUBLISHING

Chapter One

It's Saturday afternoon and Billie B. Brown is on her way to her friend Mika's house.

Billie and her friends have a brand-new mystery to solve. Mika's mom, Mrs. Okinawa, has the most beautiful patch of strawberries.

Two days ago, the plants were bursting with ruby-red fruit. But when she got home from work the next day, Mrs. Okinawa discovered that all her ripe strawberries were gone. Every single one of them!

But the most curious thing of all was that the netting she had so carefully tucked in around the strawberry plants was undisturbed. Who, or what, could have stolen all of Mrs. Okinawa's strawberries? It's a mystery, for sure!

The Secret Mystery Club are determined to uncover the truth.

The SMC has arranged to meet at Mika's house to look for clues. Billie's mom is driving Billie and Jack there. They pull up outside the house.

"See you, Mom!" Billie says as she and Jack hop out of the car. Just then, Alex's car pulls up and he gets out. The three of them walk together to the front door.

Billie whispers excitedly to Jack and Alex. "Can you believe it? Another new mystery to solve already! We must be the busiest spies in the whole neighborhood!"

"It's detectives, Billie. Remember?" Alex says, rolling his eyes. "Spies are like James Bond. Detectives are the ones that solve mysteries."

"Same thing," Billie says with a shrug, and rings the doorbell. *Sometimes Alex worries about the most unimportant details*, she thinks.

4

Mika answers the door. "Thank goodness you're here! I've been keeping Mom away from the strawberry patch all morning," she says, leading Billie and Jack through the house towards the back garden. "You know, in case she messes up any of the clues."

"Good thinking," says Alex, looking serious. "Does she suspect anyone? You know, does she have any enemies? Anyone who might want to pay her back for something?"

Billie giggles. "Alex, you watch too much TV. It's only Mrs. Okinawa's strawberries that have gone missing. Not her *jewelry*!"

Alex turns red and Billie feels a bit mean for teasing him. "But they're good ideas!" she says quickly, to make him feel a little better, even though he teased her about mixing up spies and detectives.

"No, no enemies, as far as I know," Mika says. "Mom gets along with all our neighbors."

Mika takes them through the living room towards the backyard. Billie gazes at all Mrs. Okinawa's ornaments on display.

Billie loves visiting Mika's house. Mrs. Okinawa has filled her living room with all kinds of beautiful Japanese treasures: little porcelain dolls, tiny painted plates, delicate teacups and lots of paintings of cherry blossoms.

At Mika's house there is only her and her mom, so there is nobody to break all the beautiful ornaments.

Billie knows that those little porcelain dolls wouldn't last long at her house, with Noah around!

Mrs. Okinawa is sitting at the kitchen table working at her computer. "Hi, kids!" she calls out and waves as they all trundle past.

"Hi, Mrs. Okinawa!" they call back.

"We're just going outside to play," Mika tells her mom.

They have all pinky promised not to tell anyone what they are up to.

Anything the Secret Mystery Club does is top secret!

"OK. Come back in a little while and I'll get you some snacks," Mrs. Okinawa says, smiling.

"Thanks, Mrs. Okinawa!" Billie says, **happily**. She loves the snacks Mika's mom gives them. They come in fancy packaging and they are always very sweet.

Mika opens the back door to the yard. Billie sighs with envy.

Billie's backyard is just patchy lawn, a vegetable patch, and some stinky chickens in the back. Mika's backyard is like a fairy paradise.

They walk along a white-pebbled path, between Japanese maple trees and flowering cherry trees, then past a little pond. As they pass, an enormous fish bobs up to the surface of the water and opens its mouth as if to say hello.

Billie laughs.

Soon they reach Mrs. Okinawa's strawberry patch, growing along the fence at the end of the garden.

"The scene of the crime!" Jack says **dramatically**, clutching his hand to his chest. The four of them giggle excitedly.

Billie pulls her detective things out of her backpack. The first is her secret mystery notebook with the real lock and key. The second is her magnifying glass.

The last thing is a real camera that Billie's dad lent her. Billie is going to take lots of photographs of the scene of the crime for them to study later.

Alex has brought along his voice recorder as well. He pulls it out of his pocket and turns it on. "The Secret Mystery Club's next mystery," he says into the recorder in an important voice. "Who stole Mrs. Okinawa's strawberries?" He sticks his hand out, palm down.

The others all slap their hands onto Alex's and call out loudly, "Cock-a-doodle-doooo!" into the recorder. Then Alex plays it back for them to hear and they all start **laughing**. Billie laughs the loudest of all. The Secret Mystery Club is the best fun ever!

Chapter Two

Billie puts her magnifying glass
to her eye and leans in close
to study the netting over the
strawberry patch. It is propped
up on a bamboo frame and pegged
neatly to the ground all around
the plants.

"Hmmm. I can't see any holes in the netting," she murmurs. She writes this fact down in her little book.

"Can I have a try with the magnifying glass?" Jack asks Billie. "I haven't had a turn with it yet."

"Sure," says Billie, and she hands it to him. Then she takes the camera out of its case and begins snapping pictures of the strawberry patch.

17

Mika and Alex crawl around the edge of the strawberry patch looking for clues.

"Hey, look at this!" says Mika.

The others rush over to see what she's found. There, caught in the net, is a small brown feather. Billie takes a photograph of it.

Jack studies it through the magnifying glass. "Well, it's not a magpie feather, that's for sure," he says. "If it was a magpie it would be black and white."

"It's probably a mynah," says Alex, importantly. He's the one who knows the most about birds.
Birds and math are his specialties.
"But if a bird took the strawberries, how did it get them through the net? Your mom says it hadn't been touched, Mika."

"That's true," says Mika. "But maybe its beak was small enough to poke through the holes in the net?"

Jack pokes his finger and thumb into a hole in the netting.

He takes hold of one of the pale unripe strawberries that the thief has left behind. Then he tries to pull it back through the hole in the netting. He shakes his head. "No. It won't fit," he says. "I can poke my fingers through, but the strawberries are too big to pull back out through the holes."

"Besides, birds make a big mess," says Alex. "If it was a bird that had eaten the berries there would be lots of strawberries with holes pecked in them."

"And bird poop," Billie adds, giggling. She keeps snapping photos as she talks. "There'd be poop all over the net, too."

"I think it has to be a person," Jack decides. "How else could all those strawberries have been stolen without the netting being moved? Only a person could lift up the netting and put it back again."

"I agree," Mika says. "That's exactly what I thought!"

"Well, I don't have any ideas," Alex says, stepping back and taking off his glasses to clean with his T-shirt. "I mean, how can we possibly find out who stole the strawberries? They've probably eaten them by now anyway. As Billie said, it's not like it was Mrs. Okinawa's jewelry that got stolen!"

"We can't give up yet!" Mika says. "What if it happens again?"

"Look, there are all these little baby strawberries growing now," she adds. "What if someone comes to steal them just when they get ripe, too? It's not fair!"

"Mika's right!" Billie says, putting her hand on her friend's shoulder. "We'll find out who did it, don't worry. I say we start by interviewing the neighbors. See if they saw anything or suspect anyone."

"We can't just go around to people's houses and ask if they saw a strawberry thief," Jack says.

"Why not?" says Billie.

"Well, we're supposed to be undercover, for one thing," Jack says.

"And we don't want the strawberry thief to know that we're looking for them," Mika adds. "We need to be careful."

"True," says Billie, frowning.

She rubs her forehead.

"I know!" she says, grinning. She has had a super-duper idea. "The recycling posters we made in art! We have to stick them up around the neighborhood, don't we?"

The others nod.

"We should ask Alf if we can put them up in his shop," says Billie, "and while we're there, see if we can find out some more information. He knows everyone around here."

"That's a great idea, Billie!" says Mika, looking happy again. "Let's go there tomorrow afternoon."

"Yes, let's. Bring your posters. Meanwhile, I'll upload these photos this afternoon at home and let you know if I find any more clues," Billie says, tapping her camera. Then she gives Mika a cheeky smile. "I think there's just one more thing we need to do here."

"What's that?" says Mika.

"Go inside and eat some of your mom's snacks." Billie giggles. All this talk of juicy strawberries is making her hungry!

Chapter Three

Later that afternoon, Jack comes over to Billie's house. They ask if they can use the computer to upload the photographs they took that day.

Billie closes the door to the study so that Noah can't come in.

Noah is too young for secret mystery business. Last time Billie let him come in while she was using the computer, he pushed the off button and Billie lost all her work! Even though Billie loves Noah to bits, sometimes he can be very annoying. Now, Billie can hear Noah crying outside the door because they won't let him in.

"We'll be finished soon, Nozy," Billie calls out. "Go and play with your cars."

She feels a little bit mean, but she can't play with her brother all the time. Sometimes she has important things to do!

Eventually Billie's mom takes Noah to play in the family room.

"Phew!" says Billie. "All right. Let's get to work." She plugs the camera cord into the computer and downloads the thirty-two photographs she took of Mrs. Okinawa's strawberry patch.

Most of the photos are a little blurry, which isn't very helpful, but luckily some of them are in focus. Billie opens a photograph. It is a close-up of the netting over the strawberry patch.

"Zoom in so we can see if there are any clues we missed," says Jack.

Billie zooms in, but they can't see anything unusual.

"Try another one," says Jack.

Billie zooms in on one photo after another. It takes a long time.

They study the photos carefully, but other than leaves and netting and the wood of the back fence, there is nothing very exciting to look at.

"Hmm, maybe this isn't very helpful after all," Billie says, after they have zoomed in on their twenty-seventh photograph. She is starting to get a teensy bit bored. Outside it is still sunny and she feels like going out to play.

"Just a few more," Jack says.

"We haven't looked at those ones yet." He points to the last five photographs.

"All right," Billie sighs and opens another photograph so they can study it. She shrugs. "Next?"

"No, wait!" Jack says. "Zoom in there. There. That bit by the tree. What's that?"

Billie zooms in. She gasps. There, right by the netting, is a footprint. A big boot mark in the dirt.

"We must have missed that!" Billie says excitedly. "That is definitely a clue!"

"It sure is!" Jack says happily. "That is one big footprint."

Billie nods. "Much too big to be Mrs. Okinawa's foot."

"Or Mika's!" Jack agrees.

Billie prints off the photograph with the big boot print on it. Then she turns to Jack and grins.

37

"I think if we find who this footprint belongs to, we'll find our strawberry thief!"

"Cock-a-doodle-dooooo!" the two of them crow, happily. Billie can't wait to tell the others!

Chapter Four

The next day is Sunday. The four
members of the Secret Mystery
Club meet in their tree house in
Billie's backyard. Mika has brought
a package of Japanese cookies for
them to share because she knows
they are Billie's favorite.

Billie pulls one of the long chocolate-covered sticks out of the box and chomps on it like a rabbit while the others stare at the photograph of the boot print.

She and Jack give each other a look and Billie feels her tummy bubble with excitement. She can't wait to hear what Mika and Alex have to say about the new clue they have discovered.

"Hmm. That is definitely a man's boot print," Alex says.

He is peering carefully through Billie's magnifying glass. "And there are no men living at your place, are there, Mika?"

"Nope!" says Mika confidently. She takes the magnifying glass to look at the photograph herself. "Oh, wait. There's Gus."

"Gus?" they all ask together.

"He prunes the trees. And cuts the grass." Mika shrugs. "He put the netting over the strawberries for Mom. That's probably his boot print."

"What?" says Billie, choking on her chocolate stick.

Jack looks upset, too. "Well, maybe he's the thief, Mika? He could easily lift up the netting and peg it back down without anybody knowing. Couldn't he?"

Billie and Alex nod in agreement.

"He's allergic to strawberries. He told me when he was putting the netting down," Mika says, shaking her head slowly.

43

"Sorry, guys. I guess we're back to square one."

Billie lets out a deep sigh. How disappointing! She takes another chocolate stick to make herself feel better.

Chapter Five

The Secret Mystery Club climb down from their tree house, determined to find more clues.

Jack and Alex have decided they will talk to Mika's neighbors, to ask if they saw or heard anything unusual on the night of the robbery.

Billie and Mika are going to visit Alf in his corner shop.

Alf is sure to know something, Billie thinks. Carrying rolled-up posters under their arms, she and Mika walk down the street. *Alf knows everything about everyone.*

Billie pushes open the glass door and the little bell rings. Alf comes out from the back of the shop, wiping his hands on his big grimy apron.

"Hey, kids," he says in his gruff voice. "What can I do for you?"

Billie looks at Mika. But Mika has gone quiet and her cheeks are turning pink. Billie has forgotten that sometimes Mika gets nervous talking to people she doesn't know very well.

Even though Billie knows Alf is kind, he doesn't smile much, which can make him seem a little unfriendly. So she quickly steps in front of Mika.

"Um, we've done some posters at school about saving the environment," Billie says. "We were wondering if we could put them up in your window?"

Alf points to the front of the shop. "If I take any more of your posters I won't be able to see out my own window!"

Billie and Mika turn to look. They had been so busy chatting on the way in that they hadn't paid attention to Alf's front window.

It is already full of Saving The Environment posters. Billie recognizes posters from lots of people in her class — and other classes, too.

"Sorry, kids," he says. "You'll have to find somewhere else to stick them. My window's full."

Billie sighs. This day is turning out to be full of disappointments!

"That's all right," she says glumly. "Thanks anyway, Alf."

Billie turns to walk out of the shop.
*I hope Jack and Alex are having more
luck than us!* she thinks.

"Wait!" Mika's voice comes out
as a squeak. Billie turns around in
surprise to look at Mika.

"Yes?" Alf says gruffly.

Mika's cheeks turn pinker, but she
takes a big breath and continues.
"I was just, um, wondering, who
made your jam?"

"Hmpf?" Alf says, looking puzzled.

"The strawberry jam on the counter," Mika insists. "The sign says it's homemade."

Billie feels her tummy flutter with excitement. *Go, Mika!* she thinks.

"Oh! That's Andrea," Alf says, picking up a little glass jar and turning it over in his big dry hands. "She said she made such a big batch she couldn't eat it all herself. So she dropped some off for me to sell."

"Thanks, Alf!" Mika says. "That's very helpful!" Alf looks more puzzled than ever. Mika grabs Billie's hand and the two of them dash out of the shop.

"Andrea!" Mika squeals, once they are safely outside. They dash around the corner where Alf can't see them. "The witch lady!"

"She's not a witch," Billie corrects Mika. "Remember? She's a friend of Jack's mom."

"But does she have a strawberry patch?" Mika says, a smile creeping across her face.

"Hmm. I don't think so," Billie says, trying to picture Andrea's backyard.

Mika jumps up and down on the spot. "She might not be a witch but she could be a thief!"

"You're right!" Billie says excitedly. "Come on! Let's go find the boys!"

Chapter Six

Billie and Mika find the two boys
a little way down the street.

"I think we've found the thief!"
Mika squeals.

"Really?" Jack and Alex say, looking
excited. "Who? Who?"

"Someone really scary looking…"
Mika says, giving them a clue.
"She lives in a big scary house and
has long white hair."

"Andrea?" Jack frowns. "She's not
a thief."

"She's been making strawberry
jam," Mika says. "Lots of it!
She made enough to have some
leftover for Alf to sell in his shop.
Where do you think she got all
those strawberries from, huh?"

Mika puts her hands on her hips to show that she has made up her mind. "She's our strawberry thief. I'm sure of it!"

Jack shakes his head. "I don't think it's Andrea," he mumbles. "She wouldn't do something like that."

"Only one way to find out!" Alex says, his eyes lighting up with excitement.

He and Mika run along the sidewalk towards the big scary house at the end of the street.

Billie looks at Jack. She was as excited as Mika before. She felt sure they had discovered who the thief was. But now that she sees Jack's worried expression, she's not so sure. "Come on," says Billie gently, taking Jack's hand. "Let's catch up with the others."

The four of them arrive at Andrea's house, a little out of breath. Now that they are standing in front of the big spooky house, Alex and Mika don't look as brave as before.

Billie remembers that only she and Jack have ever been inside Andrea's house. Mika and Alex have only heard about it from them.

Jack walks past them all and knocks on the door. They all stand quietly, listening to the footsteps clomping down the hall towards them. Andrea pulls open the door and blinks into the sunlight. She looks as scary as ever. Today she is wearing a long white apron with red smears all down the front of it.

Even though Billie knows there is nothing to be afraid of, Andrea still makes her shiver a bit.

"Well, well, well!" Andrea says, grinning. "You kids have arrived at the right time! I've just taken a batch of scones out of the oven to have with homemade strawberry jam. Come in! Come in!"

Mika jabs her elbow into Billie's ribs. "Thank you!" she says, her voice sounding extra brave. "I love strawberry jam!"

Then she steps past them all and follows Andrea into the house.

As they walk along the corridor, Billie can smell a sweet fruity smell coming from the kitchen. "Is that the jam I can smell?" she asks Andrea.

"Yes!" says Andrea. "My brother runs a strawberry farm and he brought me three crates of ripe strawberries yesterday."

"Oh!" says Billie, looking at Mika.

Andrea opens the door to the kitchen. There on the sticky wooden table are two empty crates covered in pink stains and one crate full of big fat strawberries.

"I knew I'd need a lot of strawberries to make jam, but I think I ordered a few too many." Andrea grins. "I've got strawberry jam coming out of my ears and I still haven't been able to use them all up. Will you kids take some home with you?"

"See?" Jack hisses in Mika's ear. Mika looks down at the floor, her cheeks turning as red as berries.

"Sit down, sit down," Andrea says, pointing to her big wooden table. "And I'll get some scones for you all. They're fresh from the oven."

Billie and her friends sit up at Andrea's kitchen table feeling downhearted. But they can't stay glum for long. Fresh scones with strawberry jam and cream is enough to cheer anybody up!

Walking back to Billie's house, swinging plastic bags full of strawberries and jam, Billie and her friends talk about their next move.

"Well, we've ruled out the neighbors," Alex says, counting people off on his fingers. "Nobody saw anyone or heard anything that night. And besides, you can't get into Mika's backyard without going through the house."

"And the back fence is too high for anyone to climb over," Jack adds.

"It wasn't birds," Alex says.

"Or any other creature," Jack says. "Otherwise the net would have been disturbed."

"It might just have to remain an unsolved mystery, Mika," Billie says kindly, draping her arm over her friend's shoulder. "We can't solve everything."

"Yes we can!" Mika says angrily. "You are all giving up too easily.

You think just because it's strawberries and not something important that was stolen, it doesn't matter. Well, it matters to me! There's a new bunch of strawberries about to ripen and I'll bet the thief will be back any day now. And it will happen again and again if we don't catch them. I thought you were my friends! I thought we were a team!"

Billie, Jack and Alex all look at Mika in shock. Mika hardly ever loses her temper.

Mika is always the quiet one. The one who lets other people make all the decisions. The one who is always happy to go along with what other people say.

Billie understands now how important it is to Mika. *That's why we can't let her down*, she thinks.

"Well, I guess there's one last thing we can try," Billie says slowly. "But it might be scary. And it will definitely be risky."

"What?" say the others, their eyes growing wide.

"We set a trap," says Billie. "To catch the thief."

The others hoot with excitement. Billie grins. She is the most excited of them all.

Chapter Seven

The Secret Mystery Club has to wait a whole week until they can put their plan into action. Every day at school they discuss the details underneath the pepper tree. Every afternoon they meet in the tree house to go over their plan.

73

Finally, the day they have been waiting for arrives. Mika's mom helps them set up Billie's tent in the backyard where they can keep a lookout over the strawberry patch.

Mrs. Okinawa is very happy to have all of Mika's friends stay the night, even if she does think it's a little strange that they all want to sleep outside. What she doesn't know is that deep inside Billie's backpack is a plastic bag full of Andrea's juicy strawberries.

When Mrs. Okinawa has gone inside, the four of them lift up the edges of the netting and scatter the ripe strawberries among the strawberry plants.

Mrs. Okinawa's own strawberries are still pale and hard, but Billie hopes that the ripe strawberries will tempt the thief to come back into the garden. If they can catch the thief that night, they might be able to save Mrs. Okinawa's next batch of strawberries.

76

The last thing Billie does before they snuggle down into their sleeping bags for the night is to attach a little bell to the netting, just like the one Alf has on his shop door. If anything or anyone disturbs the netting, they will hear the bell ringing from inside their tent.

Billie has brought along her camera. If they hear the bell she will go outside as quickly as she can and snap photos with the flash on.

It's a brilliant plan and the Secret Mystery Club are convinced they will catch their thief.

But it has been a long week and detective work is very tiring business! Billie can hear her friends' voices getting sleepy as they chat in the dark. One by one, Alex, Jack and even Mika fall asleep until Billie is the only one awake.

Her ears feel like they are almost growing bigger as she listens to the sounds outside the tent.

She hears the whisper of the wind through the leaves, the rustle of birds in the trees, even the bubble and glop of the fish in the pond. But no thief.

Billie's eyes become scratchy with tiredness. Her eyelids become as heavy as stones. Just as Billie feels herself sliding into sleep, there is a sound that snatches her eyes open.

A bell. Ding-a-ling!

There it is again!

Billie sits up and grabs her camera. She gently lifts the tent flap and points her camera towards the strawberry patch.

Flash! Flash! Flash! Her camera goes off and Billie hears a squeal and scuffle as the thief makes its getaway.

"Wake up! Wake up!" Billie tells the others, shaking them in their sleeping bags. "I got it. I got it! It's here! Look, on my camera!"

Billie switches on a flashlight as the others wake up, rubbing the sleep from their eyes. They crowd around Billie as she presses the button on the camera so they can see what she has photographed.

Billie's heart is beating so hard she can feel it in her ears. The first photograph comes on display. They see the fence, the big tree, the strawberry patch and all the netting. And there, shining out of the dark, five pairs of eyes stare back at them.

81

"I can't believe it!" Mika gasps.

The others snort with laughter.
There is not one strawberry thief,
but five! Billie zooms in and the
photograph clearly shows five
cheeky possums, their mouths
stuffed with strawberries.

Chapter Eight

At school on Monday morning, Billie, Jack and Alex are still laughing about the strawberry-stealing possums as they wait for Mika. She arrives just as the bell goes and the four of them walk to class together.

"So, did Gus fix the hole in the fence?" Alex asks Mika.

Mika grins. "He sure did! Mom called him over after you went home and he hammered a piece of wood over it. I can't believe we didn't see it there when we were looking for clues that first day."

"I guess we didn't think of looking at the fence," Jack says. "The netting was attached to it so well, who could have known there was another way in?"

"So, are you happy we caught the thieves?" Billie jokes, poking Mika in the ribs.

Mika shrugs. "Yeah, I guess. But Mom and I feel kind of sorry for the possums, too. We left some apple cores by the strawberry patch. They're probably not as yummy as strawberries, but at least the possums can still feed their babies."

"Another mystery solved!" Alex says, as they walk into class. "I wonder what will be next?"

"I hope we don't have to wait too long," Billie says happily. "We're getting pretty good at this. I'm ready to solve another one already!"

They pull up their chairs and sit down at their desks, chatting together while they wait for Mr. Benetto to arrive. It's unusual for him to be late. Usually he is already sitting at his desk when the class wanders in.

Finally, he strides into the room, his face as dark as a storm cloud.

Billie has never seen him look like this before. The rest of the class notices too, and one by one they fall quiet.

When Mr. Benetto opens his mouth to speak, his voice comes out low and angry. "I have just come from a meeting with our principal and I have some very grave news to share," he begins. "Something valuable has been taken from her office and someone in this school is responsible."

Billie feels a shiver pass through her. She glances briefly at Jack, then Mika, then Alex. She knows that none of them would dare to look back at her in case Mr. Benetto catches them, but she is certain she knows what they are thinking.

The Secret Mystery Club has another mystery to solve. And this one might be the most serious yet!

To be continued...